GARFIELD'S HAUNTED HOUSE

and other spooky tales

Created by

JIM DAVIS

Written by Mark Acey and Jim Kraft
Designed and Illustrated by Mike Fentz

PAWS, INC.

Watermill Press

Published by Watermill Press, an imprint of Troll Associates, Inc.
No part of this book may be reproduced or utilized in
any form or by any means, electronic or mechanical,
including photocopying, recording, or by any
information storage or retrieval system, without
written permission from the publisher.

Printed in the United States of America.

10 9 8 7 6 5 4 3 2 1

Contents

A GRIPPING TALE

"BOR-ING!" bellowed Garfield as he and Odie watched the fish swimming in Jon's aquarium one damp and dreary afternoon. "Back and forth, back and forth. Fish are so boring, they actually make dogs seem interesting."

Odie merely yawned.

"And these fish are so scrawny, they're not even worth eating," added Garfield. "I want to see some monstrous marine life. I want to sail 20,000 leagues under the sea like Captain Nemo, and tangle with sharks and whales and killer octopuses. I want some excitement. Of course, I'd settle for a snack."

Just then, Jon walked into the room.

"And there's my meal ticket now," remarked Garfield.

"Guess what I've got," said Jon, obviously hiding something behind his back.

"Terminal geekitis," replied Garfield.

"Doughnuts!" announced Jon, proudly displaying the bag of goodies. "Just a little something to brighten the day. Now be sure to share them."

Garfield quickly grabbed the bag. "I'll share them all right," he said. "I'll take the doughnuts, and Odie can have the holes."

With that, the furry pastry snatcher bolted out the door with Odie howling and growling in hot pursuit.

"Come back here," called Jon, halfheartedly. "Oh well, pets will be pets."

Meanwhile, the chase was on — across the soggy yard, around the flooded birdbath, through the muddy flower bed ... until at last Odie grabbed Garfield's tail, bringing the fat cat to a screeching halt.

Unfortunately, that sent the bag of doughnuts flying into the street, where it crash-landed and skidded toward an open storm sewer.

"My doughnuts!" wailed Garfield. "I've got to save them. Let go of me, you doofus dog!"

The bag was now teetering precariously on the edge of the sewer. Garfield dashed to the rescue, making a desperate lunge to snare the bag. But, alas, he was too late — the doughnuts toppled into the watery grave. Garfield's heart sank, as did his blood sugar.

"Perfectly good doughnuts down the drain," he moaned, as he peered into the mouth of the sewer. "This really stinks."

Odie frowned and nodded in agreement.

"No, I mean this *really* stinks," said Garfield, grimacing. "This sewer smells almost as bad as your breath."

"Grrrr," snarled Odie.

Garfield started to get up when he heard the rushing underground sewer water die down to a trickle. Curious, he held his nose and leaned over for a closer look. Then, without warning, the vile sewer spit out a stream of inky slosh, splattering Garfield with nasty blotches.

"Gross!" cried Garfield, cringing as he inspected his stained fur. "I look like a slimy leopard."

Odie looked on in amazement, and also with amusement.

"What are you laughing at, Hyena Face?" hissed Garfield. "This is all your fault."

Garfield reached out and grabbed Odie by the tongue, drawing him closer.

"Hey, wouldn't it be funny if I made you go fetch those drowned doughnuts?" asked Garfield menacingly. "Well, what's the matter? Cat got your tongue?"

Then, suddenly, up from the murky abyss of the sewer shot a long sucker-covered tentacle that coiled around Odie's chest.

"YYYAAAAAAAA!" yowled Odie, furiously pawing at the grotesque tentacle that was trying to pull him toward the sewer.

Garfield, still clutching Odie's tongue, instinctively tugged back.

"Don't worry, buddy! I've got you!" yelled Garfield, as Odie was being stretched to the breaking point.

But the gruesome game of tongue-of-war ended abruptly when Odie's slobbery tongue slipped through Garfield's paws, and Odie was dragged yipping and screaming down into the sewer!

"Doggone," mumbled Garfield, shaking his head in disbelief as he stared at the empty sewer. "*Now* what do I do?"

Garfield paced frantically for a moment, then stopped and took a deep breath. "Oh well, I guess a cat's gotta do what a cat's gotta do."

The tubby tabby sucked in his stomach and squeezed himself into the mouth of the sewer. He slid down its stony throat and plopped into its wet gut. Neck-deep in water and awash in darkness, Garfield struggled to make out his surroundings.

"I'm beginning to see," he said, his eyes gradually adjusting to the dark. "I'm beginning to see I'm in a heap of trouble. Where's Jacques Cousteau when you need him, anyway?"

As Garfield scanned the watery tunnel, he could see scattered rays of light slicing through the darkness from sewer gratings above the street, creating eerie images along the wall. Garfield was now shivering in the chilly air. Summoning up his courage, he called out for his missing pal.

"O-O-O-die! O-O-O-die! Can you hear me?"

A faint bark echoed in the distance.

"Hang on!" shouted Garfield. "I'm coming to save you." Then he thought, "I just wish I knew how."

But before Garfield could do anything, he felt something wrap around his waist and jerk him through the water until he was eyeball to enormous eyeball with a horrifying giant octopus!

"Boy, I bet *you* don't have any trouble reading the last line on an eye chart," said Garfield, forcing a smile. "Did I say I wanted to tangle with an octopus? I meant a platypus."

The octopus responded by hoisting Garfield and Odie into the air and conking their heads together.

"Well, this is a fine mess you've gotten us into, Odie," said Garfield, his teeth jarring, as the octopus continued to bang them together like cymbals.

Suddenly, the octopus yanked the pets close to its lethal mouth. "Uh-oh, I sense an unhappy ending," said Garfield. "This thing's armed *and* dangerous."

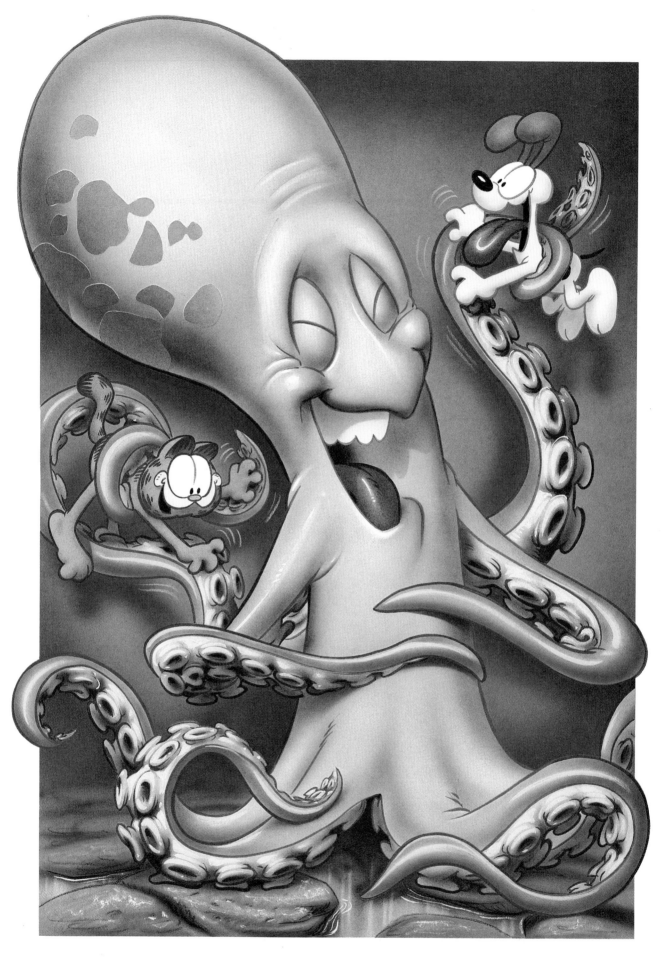

Garfield and Odie immediately intensified their efforts to escape, wriggling and writhing, clawing and biting. But the more they struggled, the tighter the tentacles squeezed, and the more its suckers latched on.

"We're running out of time ... and air!" gasped Garfield, beginning to turn blue. "I've got to do something — and fast," he thought.

Then a wild idea flashed through his mind.

"It's crazy, but who knows? It always works on Jon and Odie. Maybe desperate times call for *silly* measures — and I'm definitely scared silly."

So instead of fighting the tentacle, Garfield *tickled* it. The octopus instantly twitched.

"Quick, Odie. Lend me a paw," ordered Garfield. "If you can't beat 'em, tickle 'em."

Together, Garfield and Odie tickled the octopus unmercifully. Moments later, the octopus was flailing its tentacles and giggling like a maniac.

"It's flipped its lid," exclaimed Garfield. "Keep tickling!"

Still in the octopus's crazed clutches, Garfield and Odie were whipped through the air, then splashed into the water. With one final lurch, the octopus thrust the pets back up through the sewer hole and deposited them on the street. The two twitching tentacles disappeared amid a chorus of chortles and chuckles.

"We did it, Odie . . . old pal, old buddy," gushed Garfield. "We're safe! We're sound! We're late for dinner!"

Delighted that things were back to normal, Odie tried to embrace his friend.

"Please, no hugs," said Garfield.

Just then, Jon hollered out the window.

"Garfield! Odie! Come quick! I just saw on TV that an octopus escaped from the aquarium and is on the loose in the sewer system. It's a very serious situation."

"No kidding," said Garfield with a smile. "You might even call it a ticklish situation."

PSYCHO PIZZA

"Your pizza should be here in thirty minutes," said Jon. "I put the money on the table."

"Fine," said Garfield, without looking up from the TV. "You are dismissed."

"I'm going to take a hot bath and go to bed. Garfield, don't abuse Odie."

"I won't damage his major organs."

"And be good to Nermal. Remember, he's your guest."

Garfield cast a sour glance at Nermal, the world's cutest kitten.

"Why, I wouldn't harm Nermal," declared Garfield. "I love him to pieces. Preferably *tiny* pieces . . . that can't be identified."

Jon went into the bedroom.

"I'm really glad I could stay over," said Nermal. "So, what's on the tube tonight?"

"Well," said Garfield. "There's always the all-night cooking channel."

"Forget it," said Nermal.

"How about 'Friday Night Nightmares'?"

"Sounds pretty scary," said Nermal. "I don't really like scary movies."

"'Friday Night Nightmares' it is!" cried Garfield, flipping the channel.

"Velcome to 'Friday Night Nightmares,'" said the host, who was dressed as Count Dracula. "Tonight's feature is *Ed, The Mild-Mannered Monster.*"

Nermal peeked out from behind a sofa pillow. "Hey, that doesn't sound too scary," he said.

"Just my luck," grumbled Garfield.

The three pets settled down to watch the movie. Ed really wasn't much of a monster. He didn't growl or howl. And if he scared someone, he always politely said, "Excuse me."

"This isn't scary at all," said Nermal. "I like it."

Garfield dug his claws into the sofa. "You can never find a good monster when you need one," he moaned.

"I hope our pizza gets here soon," Nermal added.

Garfield glared at the kitten. Then, slowly, Garfield's mouth bent in a sly smile.

"I just hope our pizza isn't . . . *psycho* pizza," said Garfield.

Nermal looked at Garfield. "What are you talking about?"

"Psycho pizza. You've heard about it."

"No, I haven't."

"Nurf," added Odie, looking alarmed.

"Well, here's what *I* heard," said Garfield, leaning closer to the dog and kitten. "See, this psycho was in a special hospital because he'd done some really gross stuff to people."

"Like what?"

"It's too gross to tell. All I can say is, you don't want to be around him when he's working with power tools.

"One day, this psycho escapes from the hospital. And the police can't find him anywhere. That's because he doesn't look like a psycho. In fact, he looks completely normal, like people you pass on the street every day. Anyway, he needs money to buy some more power tools. So he gets a job. And what job do you think he gets?"

Nermal and Odie held their breath.

"Pizza delivery man."

"I was afraid of that," croaked Nermal.

"So, one night there's this teenager who's home all alone. And he gets hungry. So he orders a pizza. And who do you think delivers that pizza?"

"The psycho?" whispered Nermal.

"Bingo," said Garfield. "The kid doesn't suspect a thing. The doorbell rings. He goes to the door. He opens the door..."

"I can't look," squeaked Nermal. He covered his eyes with his paws, while Odie covered his with his ears.

Garfield paused.

Nermal peeked out. "And?"

"All the police ever found were two pieces of pepperoni and three pieces of teenager."

"Oh, gross!"

"And the worst part is," said Garfield, "they still haven't caught the psycho. He's still out there, moving around from town to town. And every now and then he makes a *special* delivery."

The doorbell rang, startling all three pets.

"That could be him right now," whispered Garfield.

"What do we *do*?" asked Nermal.

Garfield stroked his chins. "You and Odie hide in the kitchen. I'll answer the door. Whatever happens, don't come out until I call you."

Nermal and Odie hugged Garfield. "You're so brave," said Nermal.

"And you're so short," replied Garfield.

Nermal and Odie raced into the kitchen and hid in the pantry. Cowering among the canned goods, they strained to hear what was happening in the living room.

"I can't hear anything," whispered Nermal. "Maybe it wasn't the psycho after all."

The silence continued for what seemed like a long time. Then, suddenly, they heard the whine of an electric motor!

Nermal and Odie exchanged looks of terror. "Power tools!" gasped Nermal.

The noise was coming closer. It was right outside the kitchen door!

"I'm too cute to be sliced and diced!" cried Nermal.

The pantry door flew open! It was a man! A man with a tool whirring in his hand!

Nermal and Odie screamed! The man screamed! In a panic, Nermal and Odie dove between the man's legs, causing him to topple backward. Without looking back, the two pets raced through the living room and out the front door into the night!

"What's the matter?" Garfield called after them. "Don't you guys like anchovies?"

Nibbling a slice of pizza, Garfield sauntered into the kitchen.

Jon sat on the kitchen floor, gasping in surprise. His electric toothbrush vibrated on the tiles a few feet away. Jon reached over and shut it off.

"What were Odie and Nermal doing in the pantry?" asked Jon. "I was just checking to see if I have enough dog food for tomorrow. Why did they scream and run off like that?"

"Beats me," said Garfield. "Maybe they were frightened by your bunny slippers."

Jon put on his robe and went out to hunt for the frightened pets. Garfield flopped on the couch and flipped the TV to the cooking channel.

This turned out to be a fun night after all, Garfield thought, swallowing the last slice of pizza. *It just goes to show, when you order "psycho pizza," crazy things can happen!*

THE ABOMINABLE SNOWMAN

"At last!" said Jon to Garfield and Odie as he opened the door to the snowy mountain cabin he'd rented for their vacation. "We're finally getting away from it all. No smog, no noise . . ."

"No TV?!!" shrieked Garfield as he frantically looked around the sparsely furnished cabin. "No way! I've heard of roughing it, but this is cruel and unusual punishment!"

"It's everything the vacation brochure said it would be," gushed Jon. "A cozy fireplace, a wood-burning stove — the simple pleasures."

"More like a simpleton's pleasures, if you ask me," grumbled Garfield.

"And look," said Jon. "There's even an antique radio. I wonder if it works."

"Who cares?" complained Garfield. "It's not FM."

Jon fiddled with the knobs. Moments later the radio began to hum and a voice became audible through the static.

"Today's farm market report . . . pork bellies up an eighth, lard prices holding stead —" The announcer's voice broke off. There was a pause and then: **"We interrupt this program for a special bulletin. We have just received word of an unconfirmed sighting of the Abominable Snowman. We emphasize that this report is unconfirmed. However, caution is advised."**

Jon turned off the radio and said, "Isn't that the silliest thing you ever heard?"

"Better silly than sorry," said Garfield, as he and Odie peeked out from beneath a bearskin rug.

"Stop being wimps," said Jon. "Everyone knows there's no such thing as the Abominable Snowman. It's just a dumb legend. Now get out from under there and gather up some wood for the stove so I can cook dinner."

"Dinner?" chirped Garfield, salivating. "What are we waiting for?"

Garfield and Odie set off in search of firewood. Before long they came to the edge of a forest. They had taken only a few steps when Odie began yipping and pointing to something in the snow.

"Mundo bizarro!" marveled Garfield, spying what had sent Odie into an uproar. "Unless I'm insane — which is crazy — this is a footprint. A BIG footprint."

Garfield leaned over to examine the track. Just then Odie let loose an ear-piercing bark that sent Garfield shooting into the air. Instantly, a huge paw reached out and grabbed him.

"Uh, I don't suppose you're a figment of my imagination?" Garfield asked the paw's owner.

"Grrrr!" growled the Abominable Snowman.

"Well then, I don't suppose you're a vegetarian?"

"I'm sick of eating vegetables," roared the Snowman, baring his sharp, yellow teeth.

"That's good," said Garfield, "because I'm a carrot. Yeah, that's it — a big furry carrot."

The Snowman was not amused. He opened his mouth and dangled Garfield over his cavernous jaws.

"Wait!" cried Garfield. "You've got to grant me a last request. That's the way it's done in the movies."

"Huh?" said the Snowman. "Duh, okay. What is it?"

"What else? Don't eat me!" said Garfield. "Looks like I got you on a technicality, Snowball Brain. You've *got* to let me go."

The Snowman thought a minute, then lowered Garfield to the ground.

"The bigger they are, the dumber they are. He's almost as stupid as a dog," mumbled Garfield. "So tell me, Snowman — or should I call you Abominable? — how did you get your name?"

"Uh, my real name is 'Yeti.' They call me the Abominable Snowman because I'm always so abominable. You know, ravaging the countryside and stuff like that."

"But why are you so abominable?" asked Garfield.

"I'm always in a bad mood because I'm always freezing. It's not easy living out here in the snow!" snapped Yeti.

"I think I see your problem," said Garfield. "You don't have a hat."

"A hat?" asked Yeti.

"Yeah, a hat," repeated Garfield. "Every snowman needs a hat. Don't you know anything? Eighty percent of your body heat escapes through your head. So if you cover it up, you'll keep warm. And besides, girls really go for guys in hats. Why, the snow babes will be crawling all over you."

"They will?" said Yeti. "Then I want a hat! Gimme a hat!"
Suddenly, he snatched Garfield up.

"You'd make a nice hat," said the Snowman as he stretched Garfield into different shapes.

"Chill out, you big doofus," squealed Garfield. "I'll get you a hat — a *real* hat. Just let me go. And if I'm not back in ten minutes, you can make Odie into a hat."

"Hunh?" gulped Odie.

"Trust me," said Garfield. "Have I ever let you down?"

Odie cupped his head in his paws and began to whine. Finally, the Snowman agreed and set Garfield down. Off Garfield zoomed toward the cabin. Slipping and sliding, huffing and puffing, he ran as fast as a fat cat can.

"Gotta get a hat," he thought. "Gotta save Odie. Gotta stop saying, 'gotta.'"

Skidding to a halt when he reached the cabin, Garfield peeked through a window. There sat Jon warming his feet by the fire. Garfield didn't see a hat, but he did see Jon's long thermal underwear hanging on a peg near the door.

"Beggars can't be choosers," he thought, nudging open the door and swiping the long johns.

Racing back to the forest, Garfield could only hope that Odie wasn't a poochskin cap by now. At last he spotted the Snowman — and Odie — safe and sound.

"Check it out," panted Garfield, displaying Jon's long johns. "The latest thing in headgear."

Yeti hesitated, then snatched the long johns and yanked them on his head.

"It's hot . . . it's cool . . . it's *you!*" praised Garfield, laying it on thick.

A big smile crept over the Snowman's face.

"Now maybe you could do us a favor," said Garfield. "Odie and I were supposed to bring back some firewood."

The Snowman unleashed a flurry of karate chops, transforming an old, fallen tree into a woodpile.

"Thanks. Paul Bunyan couldn't have done it better," said Garfield. "Well, we're outta here. Stay cool — uh — make that *warm!*"

Yeti grinned and patted his hat. Then he waved good-bye.

Soon Garfield and Odie arrived at the cabin with the firewood.

"What took you so long? I thought maybe the Abominable Snowman got you," cackled Jon.

"Get real. There's no such thing as the Abominable Snowman," said Garfield, winking at Odie. "At least, not anymore. Now he's nice."

IS THERE A SPECTER
IN THE HOUSE?

The moon shone through the broken window, causing the monster's eyes to glow an evil green. The rough hairs on its back bristled with menace. Yellow fangs protruded from its ugly mouth. As the thing uncoiled its long, sinister legs and crept across the floor, Garfield's face twisted with fear. What should he do? Should he run? Should he scream?

The thing crept closer and closer. It was nearly on him! And then . . .

WHAM! Garfield smashed the monster into a hairy glob of goo!

"Garfield!" cried Jon, nearly dropping his camera and flashlight. "Stop squishing those spiders! You're making Odie and me nervous!"

"Spiders make *me* nervous," replied Garfield. "And this musty old house is like a spider resort. I mean it. I've seen spiders

wearing shorts and carrying little suitcases. It's a good thing I found this spider whacker."

Garfield tapped the old table leg three times on the dusty floor . . . and heard three taps in reply!

"Uh, that knocking is a good sign, right?" asked Jon, looking around anxiously. "It means this house really *is* haunted."

"It means you have cobwebs for brains," replied Garfield. "There are no ghosts in this house. There are no ghosts anywhere. Let's go home. The TV misses me."

"I hope I get a good picture," Jon continued, checking his camera. "*Supernatural News* is offering $10,000 to anyone with an authentic photograph of a ghost."

"I told you, Jon — there are no such things as ghosts. If the magazine people want something weird, send them a picture of Odie. Now, let's go home."

Garfield tried to drag Jon out of the house, but without success. "I'm not leaving until I get a picture of a ghost," Jon insisted.

Jon led his two pets deeper into the dark hallways of the old house. Carefully, they peeked into rooms and closets. Once they opened a door and heard a horrible screech! A bat zoomed out of the closet, forcing the three ghost-hunters to hit the floor!

"It's a vampire!" cried Jon.

"Not!" said Garfield. "The only pain in the neck around here is *you*!"

A short time later, they peered into a room . . . and saw mysterious white shapes floating in the dark!

"Ghosts!" cried Jon, his camera flashing.

"Yip!" said Odie, leaping into Garfield's arms.

"There are no ghosts!" croaked Garfield. "Unfortunately, these ghosts didn't get the message!"

Garfield tried to pry Odie's paws from around his neck. "Don't be such a scaredy dog!" he said. "Go drool on the ghouls!"

But the ghosts didn't come near the terrified trio. In fact, they didn't move at all.

"Wait a minute," said Garfield. "I smell a phony phantom." He dropped Odie, walked up to one of the ghosts, and gave a yank. A sheet came away in his hand.

"Well, what do you know," said Jon. "It's just some old furniture covered with sheets. We'll have to keep hunting." He stepped carefully down the hallway, with Odie trembling right behind.

Alone now, Garfield drummed his fingers impatiently on his tummy. "I want to go home," he said to himself. "I want my bed. I want my teddy bear. I want breakfast cereal that tastes like lasagna. I want lots of things. But I'm not going to get any of them until Jon gets his ghost!"

Garfield kicked at the sheet lying on the floor. Then he picked it up. Slowly, his frown turned to a sly grin. With his claw, Garfield poked two large eye holes in the sheet. Then he put it over his head. "If Jon wants a ghost, I'll give him a ghost," he said.

Unaware that Garfield was no longer behind them, Jon and Odie were about to check out the second floor of the house, when suddenly they heard a chilling sound.

"WHOOOOOOOOOOO!"

"What was that?" said Jon. Odie whimpered and hid behind Jon's legs.

A short, fat phantom appeared at the top of the stairs.

"WHOOOOOOOOOOO again!" it said, waving its arms.

"A ghost!" cried Jon. Quickly aiming his camera, he began taking pictures. The ghost stopped moaning and started posing.

Jon snapped photos until he was out of film. "I did it, boys!" he cried. "The money's mine! Now let's get out of here!"

Jon and Odie raced out the door and tumbled into Jon's car.

"Wait!" shouted Garfield through his sheet. "Don't leave yet! You didn't get my best side!" Garfield started down the stairs, but his foot got tangled in the sheet. *Bump, bump, bump!* The fat cat bounced like a basketball down the stairs. By the time he rolled to a stop, Jon and Odie were gone.

Garfield dusted himself off. "Well *that* worked perfectly," he grumbled, "except for the part where I break every bone in my body and have to spend the night in this spider factory! And it's all Jon's fault! He's so gullible. How can anyone believe in ghosts?!"

"It's a mystery to us," said a strange voice.

Garfield jerked his head around. Floating behind him were two grinning ghosts!

"Do *you* believe in ghosts?" said one ghost to the other.

"Of course not," the other replied. "Do you?"

"Don't be silly. I'm just a figment of my imagination." The ghost turned to Garfield. "What do *you* believe, kitty?"

"I . . . I . . . I believe I hear the refrigerator calling!" said Garfield. And he bolted out the door and ran away.

The ghosts watched the fat cat disappear into the night.

One phantom shook his head. "So many people don't believe in us," he observed, sadly. "It's not easy being a ghost."

"That's true," said the other. "But if you're dead, it's a pretty good living!"

Roaring with laughter, the two ghosts floated up the stairs.